Gloria Sobel
2006

Jacob & His Magical Flying Bears

written by Gerrie Sobel

illustrated by Dottie Torres

the Peppertree Press

Sarasota, Florida

ISBN: 978-1-934246-00-9
Library of Congress Number: 2006936401
Printed in the U.S.A.
First Edition Printed October, 2006

Dedication

"To my darling, precious, Grandson, Jacob,
who was truly my inspiration for writing this book".

Acknowledgements

First and foremost I would like to say Thank You to my family Joel, Jack, Kim and of course, Jacob, for all of their support during this new adventure in my life! I would also like to thank the Staff of The Peppertree Press, Julie Ann Howell, Publisher and President, as well as, Vern Firestone, Director of Creative and Marketing Services. This book would not be possible, if it were not for both their belief in the book, as well as, their time and talent. A special thank you definitely goes to Dottie Torres, who captured my vision so perfectly, with her wonderful illustrations! Many thanks go to my cousin, Joseph Polizzi, Ph.d, who was both my mentor and helped cheer me on, each and every step of the way. Thank you also to Aimee Johnson who diligently helped me send the manuscript out to various publishing houses. A special note of thanks goes to my attorney, John Donsbach, who gave me the courage to take a leap of faith and believe in myself. Finally, thank you to all of my friends and family, who jumped on the band wagon and actually bought the book!

Jacob and His Magical Flying Bears

There once was a little boy named Jacob who lived in the tiny Village of Cabbagetown. Jacob was six years old and soon to be seven on December 25th. Christmas was Jacob's favorite holiday because it was his birthday as well. However, this year, Jacob was very upset because he could not visit Santa Claus at the mall due to the fact that he had been sick with the flu. Jacob was so sad because he needed to tell Santa what he wanted for Christmas. He was sure Santa would forget all about him. He worried and worried because there was something special that he wanted, but there was no way to tell Santa. Mommy said to send Santa a letter, which Jacob did, but would Santa get it in time?

$\mathcal{E}$arly on Christmas Eve, Mommy was putting Jacob to bed and tucking him in. She said she was glad his temperature was back to normal. But all Jacob could think of was that it was too late to see Santa! Mommy said good night and then said that she was switching on Jacob's magical flying bears, which flew above his bed. She said to watch the bears because they flew to special magical places. Jacob loved watching his bears because they helped put him to sleep. He also knew that real bears didn't fly; only birds and planes could fly. But still he wished that the bears were real so that he could hop on their backs and fly to the North Pole and see Santa.

Jacob wanted lots of things for Christmas, such as a new bike, a soccer ball, a fire truck, and, oh yes, a puppy dog! (After all, it was his birthday, too!) But more than any of these things, he wanted one very important thing, and only Santa could get it done. If Santa could do this one thing, Jacob would be happy to give up all of the toys, including the puppy dog!

As Jacob was about to go to sleep, he thought he saw one of the bears above his bed wink at him. Jacob thought he must be dreaming! And then he thought he saw the second bear wink as well. And finally, he saw the third bear wink! He couldn't believe his eyes. The bears were winking and smiling at him. And then in a flash, they were all standing around his bed!

The first bear said, "Hi, my name is Speedy Bear, and I can take you anywhere in the world in a flash."

The second bear said, "Hi, my name is Pokey Bear. I'm not quite as fast as Speedy, but I can take you all around your town so that you can see all of the special things that are happening before Christmas."

The third bear said, "Hi, my name is Honey Bear. I'm the bear who will get you back safely to your home and tuck you in bed before Christmas morning."

Speedy was the first to say, "Well, Jacob, we know what you have been wishing for, and we are here to help make your wish come true. Are you ready for the ride of your life? Because we are all taking you to the North Pole to see Santa Claus! Jacob could not believe his eyes, or ears, for that matter. Would it be okay with his mom? The bears assured Jacob that when Mommy got up in the morning to wake Jacob, he would be asleep in his bed, right where she tucked him in. Honey Bear suggested that Jacob put on his snowsuit and boots, as well as a warm cap and muffler because where they were headed was very cold!

The next thing Jacob knew, he was flying on the back of Speedy, out his bedroom window with Pokey and Honey bears trailing behind. Off they all went, past the big dipper and a full moon. All of the stars were twinkling in the night sky as they flew by.

First they took a quick ride around the world so that Jacob could see all of the countries that celebrated Christmas. Then they headed for the North Pole. The first thing they saw as they landed was a magical village filled with busy elves running here and there. Santa's sleigh was parked outside of his workshop with eight tiny reindeer ready to take him on his annual ride.

They were greeted at the front door of Santa's house by Mrs. Claus, who invited them into her kitchen, which smelled of chocolate, peppermint, and gingerbread all at once! She immediately recognized Jacob, which surprised him. Mrs. Claus invited Jacob and the bears to sit down for some fresh hot gingerbread cake and hot chocolate. Then she told Jacob that Santa would be right down to have a chat with him.

All of a sudden, Jacob heard a "Ho, ho, ho" coming down the stairs to the kitchen. Jacob also heard Santa say, "Where's my little magical flying bears and Jacob? Why, there you are!" Santa joined Mrs. Claus, Jacob, and the bears around the big table. Then he told Jacob never to worry about not being able to see Santa at the mall. Santa wanted Jacob to know that the very first stops he makes in every city are at the hospitals and homes where children are sick. He also wanted Jacob to know that he was glad that Jacob was feeling better and that by tomorrow, he would be perfectly fine! That made Jacob feel much better, but he still seemed so sad. Santa asked Jacob to come over to his magic chair and sit on his lap and tell Santa what it was that he wanted for Christmas.

Jacob decided to whisper in Santa's ear because he was afraid that if he said it out loud, it would not come true. Santa looked serious for a moment. Then he told Jacob that his wish was a difficult one, but not impossible. He said he would have to talk to one of his Generals about this. Generals? Jacob didn't know that Santa had any Generals! Santa assured Jacob that he would do everything he could to make his wish come true, but there wasn't a lot of time left.

Santa gave a wink and a nod to the magical flying bears, which meant it was time for them to take Jacob back home to the village of Cabbagetown. Jacob thanked Santa and Mrs. Claus for everything and said that this was the most exciting night of his life. Jacob hopped on Speedy's back, and out the window they flew. Jacob thought, *Doesn't anyone use doors anymore?* In a flash, they were back in Jacob's hometown. Speedy said to Jacob that Pokey would take over now. So Jacob hopped on Pokey's back and flew all over Cabbagetown.

The first stop was to Mr. Freshly's Cabbage and Tree Farm, where people were still buying Christmas trees. Jacob was always surprised to see how many people waited till the last minute to buy a Christmas tree. Why, Jacob's mom put up their Christmas tree right after Thanksgiving! Jacob also noticed that Mr. Freshly's truck was full of Christmas trees. Every Christmas Eve, he would close early so that he could deliver Christmas trees to families who could not afford to buy one. As Mr. Freshly was saying good-bye to his last customer, Jacob noticed a familiar wink and a nod!

The next stop was to peek in the kitchen of Mrs. McSweet, who was baking her famous Christmas cookies. Her kitchen reminded Jacob of Mrs. Claus' kitchen. Jacob couldn't wait till Christmas morning, when Mrs. McSweet would stop by with a plate of her delicious cookies. He especially loved her gingerbread men! Mrs. McSweet would not only deliver cookies to Jacob and his family, but to all of the families in their neighborhood. She also took boxes of her homemade cookies to all of the homeless shelters, where Jacob knew there would be children waiting for her treats.

The last stop was Jacob's church, where the children's choir was practicing for midnight mass. The church looked beautiful with candles lit everywhere. And there in the manger was the real reason why people celebrate Christmas. Jacob knelt down and said a prayer. Jacob felt very special to have been born on the same day.

It was now time to go home, so Jacob hopped on Honey Bear's back, and away they flew to Jacob's home. They flew into Jacob's bedroom (through the window, of course), and Honey Bear tucked Jacob in bed. She said good night to Jacob, gave him a kiss on the cheek, and then took her place above his bed, along with Speedy and Pokey. As they flew above the bed, Jacob became very sleepy and finally fell into a deep, deep sleep.

Late on Christmas Eve

The general was busy at his desk when the Lieutenant came in to announce, "Sir, he's here." The General stopped what he was doing and listened to the noises above him on the roof. Then suddenly, there was a loud thump in the fireplace, and the jolly old elf was before him. "Santa," the General said, "I have been expecting you!"

Still Later That Night

Santa arrived back at his sleigh after his meeting with the general. He looked down at the tiny village and was very sad indeed. There was a tear in Santa's eye, which he quickly wiped away. He said to his team of reindeer, "I need you to perform your magic tonight! We are going into dangerous territory, but we are going to make a lot of children very happy!" He also remembered his promise to Jacob.

Christmas Morning

Jacob's mom came in and woke Jacob up. "Jacob, it's time to get up. It's Christmas morning, darling! Oh, how silly, I left your mobile of magical flying bears on all night. I must have been quite sleepy last night!" Jacob was now wide awake. He couldn't wait until he got downstairs to see if his special gift had arrived.

When Jacob reached the living room, there was a shiny new two-wheeler bike waiting for him. And, oh my gosh, there was the new soccer ball, and wow, look at the huge red fire engine! Jacob's mom had another surprise for him. She handed him a basket that had a top on it. He lifted the top, and out came the cutest little puppy he had ever seen. It was a little white Labrador retriever, and he immediately named it Mollie. Jacob was so happy with all of his toys and his new puppy.

Then Jacob handed his mom a small gift. It was a silver heart on a chain that Jacob had bought for her at his school's Christmas bazaar! He had emptied out his piggy bank so that he would have a gift for his mom. She loved it and gave Jacob a kiss on the cheek. But Jacob realized very quickly that Santa had not been able to get him the one thing he really wanted. As Jacob looked at his mom, he could sense that she, too, wanted that one special gift. He even noticed tears in her eyes.

At that very moment, the front door swung open, and in walked Jacob's dad, who had been fighting in a war far, far away. Daddy was a captain in the Army, and he had been gone for more than a year!

Jacob's dad stood there looking so handsome in his uniform with all of his medals. His arms were full of packages and gifts, which he dropped on the floor when he saw Jacob and his mom. Jacob ran to the door, as did his mom. They were all crying and laughing at the same time. His mom's tears were now tears of joy! She kept saying that she couldn't believe it. This was the gift that Jacob had wanted to give to his mom. This was definitely going to be the best Christmas ever and a very happy birthday for Jacob! And Santa made it happen, along with a little help from Jacob's magical flying bears!

Jacob looked out the window and up at the sky and whispered, "Thank you, Santa, for bringing my daddy home!"

Late on Christmas Night

After a wonderful day of just being with his daddy, whom Jacob had missed so much, and eating Mommy's wonderful Christmas dinner and enjoying Mrs. McSweet's delicious cookies and playing with his new puppy, it was finally time to go to bed!

This time Daddy carried Jacob on his back and Mommy tucked him in bed. After a wonderful bedtime story, they both kissed Jacob. Jacob's mom then turned on the mobile above his bed and said that she was going to switch on Jacob's magical flying bears. Mommy reminded Jacob that bears really couldn't fly (only birds and planes could fly)! Daddy just chuckled. Then they said good night and walked out of the room.

Jacob looked up at his three magical flying bears. They all winked at him, and Jacob winked right back!

The End

About the Author

Gerrie Sobel is a Certified Trainer of Food & Beverage Sales & Service and has an extensive background in the Hospitality Business for over 30 years.

From 1990-98 she served as both Innkeeper and Food & Beverage Sales manager for the historic Partridge Inn in Augusta, Georgia. During that time period, Gerrie was an active member of Women in Business, served as a Senior Advisor to the Junior League and served on Committees for the Festival of Trees Celebration.

When she and her husband moved to Florida, Gerrie developed an Employee Orientation Program for Seaside Community Development Corporation. "Excellence in Service" was developed for both the Retail as well as the Food & Beverage Outlets of Seaside.

Prior to returning to Augusta, she and her husband Joel were instrumental in helping their son Jack open a restaurant in Atlanta, called Agave. Jack, is now the successful owner of two restaurants in Atlanta, Agave and Redfish.

Presently, Gerrie continues to work side by side, with Joel, who is COO of The Pinnacle Club. She contnues to train staff and is the Special Events Director for the Club. In recent years, she also served on the Board of Safe Homes.

Jacob and His Magical Flying Bears came from her inspiration when her Grandson Jacob was born. The book was written in his honor.

About the Illustrator

Dottie Torres recently graduated from the Ringling School of Art and Design with a BFA in Illustration. When she is not doodling and painting she enjoys sewing and making costumes. Dottie has recently finished her first book *Jacob and his Magical Flying Bears* and is working towards becoming an accomplished childrens book illustrator. She currently lives in New Port Richey with her husband and three pet cacti (because she's allergic to dogs).

ISBN-13: 978-1-934246-00-9
ISBN-10: 1-934246-00-X

90000

9 781934 246009